W9-ARQ-686

READER COLLECTION

FUN WITH Clifford

by Norman Bridwell

Scholastic Inc.

The author would like to thank Manny Campana, Grace Maccarone, and Frank Rocco for their contributions to these books.

ISBN 978-0-545-92621-8

10 9 8 7 6 5 4 3 2 16 17 18 19 20

Printed in China 38
First printing 2015

Clifford's Class Trip

Emily Elizabeth's class is going on a trip today.

Clifford comes, too.

SCHOOL BUS

Some girls and boys ride the bus.
Some ride Clifford.

They are ready to learn about
animals from the sea.

First they see seals.

A seal hits a ball.

Clifford hits it back.

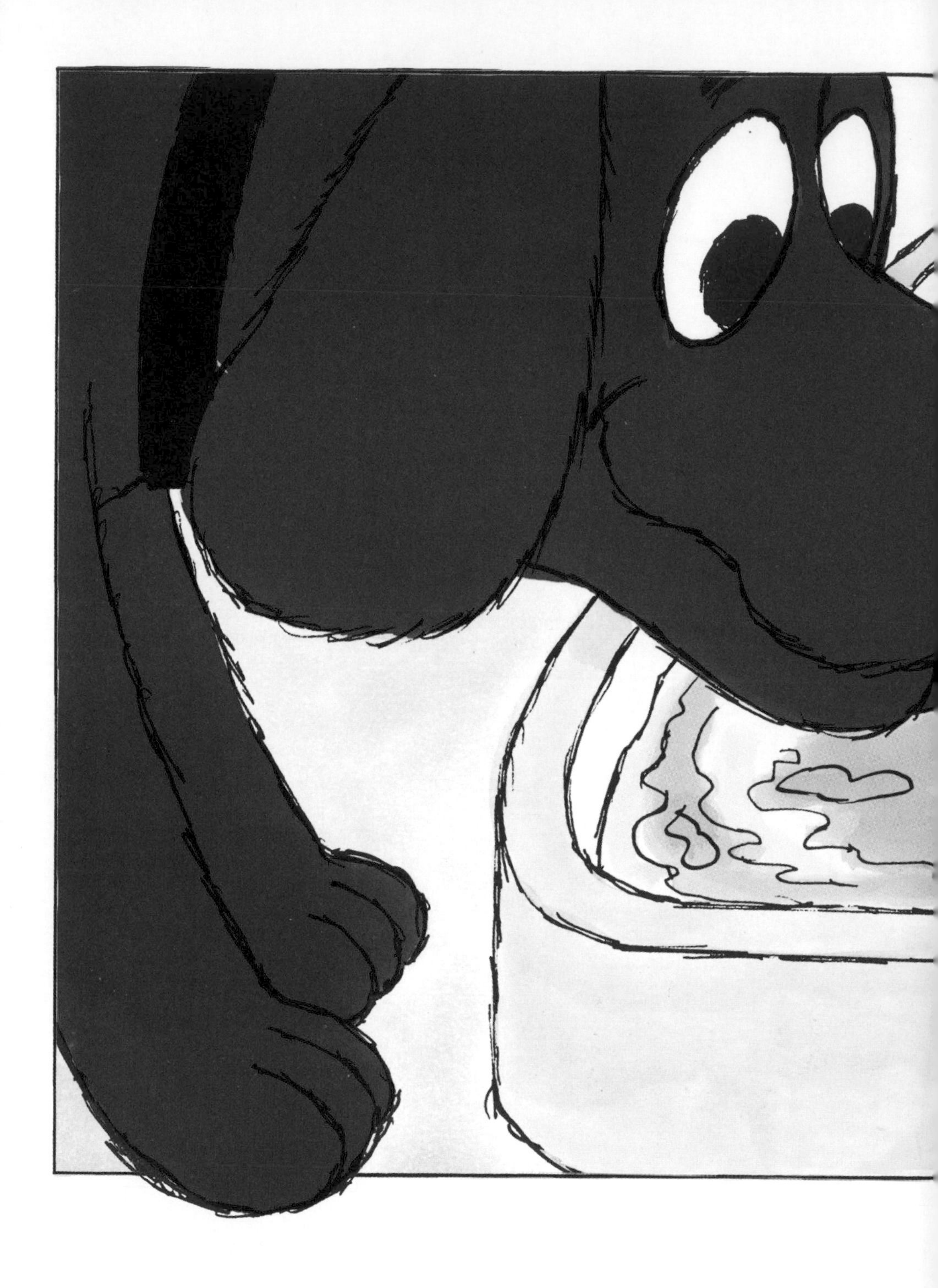

They go to the next tank.
What is this?
Clifford wants to know.

Uh-oh! He gets too close.

A friend comes to help.

Clifford says thanks.

Then Clifford sees a baby whale.

The whale needs to go
back to the ocean.
But the truck won't start.

Can you guess who can help?

Clifford can!

Clifford carries the children
and the whale.

At the dock, they get on a boat.

Soon they are far out in the bay.

The little whale is home.

Big whales come to meet her.

And Clifford makes some
new friends!

It was the best class trip ever!

Clifford's
Best Friend

This is Clifford's best friend.
Her name is Emily Elizabeth.

She wakes up early
in the morning.

She says hello to Clifford.

She eats breakfast.

Then she feeds Clifford breakfast.

Clifford takes Emily Elizabeth
to school.

Clifford cannot go inside school.
He stays outside.

After school, Clifford takes
some friends for a ride.

Then Emily Elizabeth does
her homework.

Now her homework is done.
Emily Elizabeth and her friends
play with their dogs.

The dogs like to play catch.
Clifford wants to play catch, too.

No, Clifford.
That is not a stick.
That is a tree.

Clifford puts the tree back.
Good dog, Clifford.

Clifford thinks he sees a big Frisbee.
He wants to catch it.

Clifford catches the Frisbee.
He puts it down.

Look! Purple aliens!

It isn't a Frisbee after all!

The aliens see Clifford.
Then they fly away fast.

Clifford and Emily Elizabeth eat dinner.

After dinner, Emily Elizabeth
gets ready for bed.

She says good night to her big red dog.

Then she dreams sweet dreams.

Emily Elizabeth loves Clifford.
He is her best friend!

Clifford's Busy Week

Clifford loves his toy mouse.

But where is it?

It is not in the doghouse.

It is not in the people house.

Clifford wants to find his toy.
He will look for it every day this week.

On Sunday, Clifford goes
to the playground.

The toy mouse is not there.

It is not there.

On Monday, Clifford goes to the market.

His toy is not there.

Clifford is crying.

On Tuesday, Clifford goes to the fun park.

The toy mouse is not on the ride.

It is not in the fun house.

It is not at the game.

On Wednesday, Clifford goes to the farm.

His toy mouse is not in the barn.

His toy mouse is not with the chickens.
Ah-choo! Feathers make Clifford sneeze.

On Thursday, Clifford goes to the gym.

His toy is not there.

On Friday, Clifford goes to the lake.

The toy mouse is not in the boats.

It is not under the boats.

Dad gives Clifford a new toy mouse.
Clifford does not want it.

On Saturday, Dad plays golf.
Is the toy mouse in the hole?

Clifford digs and digs.

His mouse is not there.

Later, Clifford goes to Grandma's house.
He is very sad.

“Here is your mouse,” says Grandma.
“You left it here last week.”

Clifford thanks Grandma.

He is happy now!

Clifford
Makes the Team

It is a sunny day.
Clifford wants to play.

Clifford sees a boy.
He has a bat.

Clifford sees a girl.
She has a bat, too.

Clifford follows
them to the park.

BALL
FIELD

The children play ball.

They have fun.
Clifford wants to play, too.

Clifford looks for a bat.

He sees a tree.

Can he use that as a bat?

No. The tree has branches.

Clifford puts it back.

Clifford sees a pole.
Can he use that as a bat?

SLOW

No. The pole has wires.

Clifford puts it back.

Clifford sees a pipe.
Can he use that as a bat?

No. The workers do not want
Clifford to take the pipe.

Clifford puts it back.

Clifford goes back
to watch the game.

He is sad. He is crying.
The boys and girls are
getting wet.

A boys says,
"I think Clifford wants to play."

The boys and girls want
Clifford to play.
They make up a new game.
They call it Clifford baseball.

The boys and girls hit and pitch.
Clifford plays first base, second base,
third base, and shortstop.

Clifford plays left field,
center field, and right field.

Everyone wins with Clifford!